ENDGAME

Published by Barrington Stoke
An imprint of HarperCollins*Publishers*
1 Robroyston Gate, Glasgow, G33 1JN

www.barringtonstoke.co.uk

HarperCollins*Publishers*
Macken House, 39/40 Mayor Street Upper,
Dublin 1, DO1 C9W8, Ireland

First published in 2026

Text © 2026 Melinda Salisbury
Cover design and illustration © 2026 Holly Ovenden

The moral right of Melinda Salisbury to be identified
as the author of this work has been asserted in accordance
with the Copyright, Designs and Patents Act, 1988

ISBN 978-0-00-875035-0

10 9 8 7 6 5 4 3 2 1

All rights reserved. No part of this publication may be reproduced, stored in a retrieval system, or transmitted, in whole or in any part in any form or by any means, electronic, mechanical, photocopying, recording or otherwise without the prior permission in writing of the publisher and copyright owners

Without limiting the exclusive rights of any author, contributor or the publisher of this publication, any unauthorised use of this publication to train generative artificial intelligence (AI) technologies is expressly prohibited. HarperCollins also exercise their rights under Article 4(3) of the Digital Single Market Directive 2019/790 and expressly reserve this publication from the text and data mining exception

A catalogue record for this book is available from the British Library

Printed and bound in India by Replika Press Pvt. Ltd.

This book contains FSC™ certified paper and other controlled
sources to ensure responsible forest management.

For more information visit: www.harpercollins.co.uk/green

EndGame

WILL TAKE YOU DOWN

MELINDA SALISBURY

Barrington Stoke

THE STORY SO FAR ...

Ruby Brooks, Freya Dixon and Ivy Finch quickly became friends when they met at Chalmers Hall. They were there to attend a summer camp for teenagers who needed a detox from technology. The camp was hosted by the Ash Tree Foundation, an organisation that claimed to help teenagers addicted to technology.

Aspiring actor Ruby had been stalked and almost killed after she'd downloaded the EchoStar app to help her with her schoolwork.

Wannabe eco-influencer Freya had become a criminal when she followed the advice of the AdelAIDE home assistant to try to boost her social media profile.

And keen gamer Ivy was sent to the Ash Tree Foundation after arranging to secretly meet up with a fellow gamer. Ivy realised he had lied about his age when he'd tried to lure her into his car.

The girls thought they'd be spending their school holiday learning to be less dependent on technology. It was looking as if it was going to be a pretty boring summer ...

Instead, they discovered the Ash Tree Foundation was a front for Novo Reality, a dangerously addictive augmented-reality platform. This was the brainchild of tech-baroness Dagmar Nilsson, who dreamed of a world where everyone was constantly logged in to Novo Reality and under her control. Dagmar worked with her nephew, famous influencer Conrad O'Connell, to isolate Ivy from the other girls and convince her to join Novo Reality.

Ivy was hidden away in a folly in the grounds of Chalmers Hall and hooked up to an augmented-reality machine 24/7. Meanwhile, Dagmar told everyone Ivy had run away, leaving her parents and friends frantic and terrified.

But Ruby and Freya didn't believe their new friend had run away. They discovered the truth as they tried to find clues about where Ivy might have gone: Dagmar Nilsson and the Ash Tree

Foundation were behind EchoStar and AdelAIDE, and now Ivy was in terrible danger too.

They managed to rescue her, despite all three girls almost being killed in the process. But Dagmar and Conrad escaped ...

Now, a year later, their lives are mostly back to normal. Freya is about to move to Scotland to start university, and Ruby and Ivy are preparing to start sixth form when the summer holidays are over.

But Dagmar Nilsson hasn't given up her dreams of ruling the world through technology just yet ...

CHAPTER 1

I lay on Freya's bed and peered around her bedroom. You couldn't tell Freya was leaving for Scotland in the morning unless you looked very carefully and knew her very well.

The thing was, I *did* know Freya very well. Since surviving our ordeal at the Ash Tree Foundation, we'd become really good friends, so I could easily spot all the things Freya had packed to take to university in Scotland.

For example, a photo of me, Freya and Ruby was missing from the corkboard above Freya's desk. We'd asked a theatre usher to take it when we saw *Hadestown* in London last Christmas. The three of us had squashed together to fit the poster of Hermes behind us into the shot. My cheek had been mashed against Ruby's face, with Freya squeezed in on Ruby's other side and Hermes smirking over our heads.

Also missing was Freya's battered old sewing machine. Freya's stepsister, Ella, had told Freya not to pack it because there wasn't space for it in the tiny flat Freya would be sharing with Ella and Ella's girlfriend, Margot.

This wasn't the same Margot who'd shown me how to use Novo Reality in the folly of the grounds of Chalmers Hall; it was just a weird coincidence they had the same name *and* both worked in technology. Ella's Margot was a website developer and definitely not in a creepy cult. Still, it made me shudder every time someone said her name, and I'd asked Freya to refer to her as "Ella's Margot" to help me out.

Anyway, Freya declared she'd sleep under the bed and keep the sewing machine on top of it if she had to, so Ella gave in and let her pack it.

The wardrobe had been cleared out too. I hauled myself off the bed and walked over to it, hitting at the empty hangers like a bored cat.

"What are you doing?" Freya asked me as she entered the room.

"Ivy's moping," Ruby said, coming in behind Freya.

"I am not," I said. "You can't even see my face because it's looking at the wardrobe."

"Yes, but I can sense it," Ruby replied. "I'm very sensitive to moods."

Ruby pushed past Freya and came to stand in front of me with her arms folded.

Then she sniffed the air around my head. "Yup," she declared. "Moping."

"I am *not*," I said.

"I'll be back at Christmas," Freya said. "And we'll message all the time."

"I just don't understand why you're going now," I said before I could stop myself. "We have the whole summer holiday left. University doesn't even start until the end of September."

"To settle in," Freya and Ruby said together, then laughed.

"I know, I know," I added, trying to summon a smile. "I'll just miss you, that's all. I'll miss us all together. Last summer was awful. I really hoped we'd have a great summer this year."

The three of us went silent as we remembered what happened to us last year at Chalmers Hall.

"It might still be a great summer?" Freya said, but she didn't sound convinced.

I tried to imagine what tomorrow would be like without Freya around, and the day after, and the day after that.

"No!" Ruby shouted suddenly, making me and Freya jump. "We're not doing this. Not on Freya's last night. Come on – let's go out and get gelato or something."

"Gelato?" I said, giving Ruby a puzzled look. "Where would we get gelato in this town?"

"I also said 'or something'," Ruby huffed. "Now let's go!"

*

We didn't find gelato, but we did find tubs of fancy ice cream in a takeaway pizza place a few streets away. We got one chocolate and one cherry, passing them between each other as we walked. It was a warm night, the beginning of summer, and we wandered aimlessly. Ice cream dribbled down our faces as we laughed at Ruby's jokes.

Until a pair of gates loomed in front of us.

"Chalmers Hall," Freya said in a low voice.

I hadn't been back here since the night Freya and Ruby rescued me from Dagmar Nilsson and the Ash Tree Foundation. None of us had.

One of the gates was hanging off its hinges. They stood open like an invitation.

"Let's go home," Freya said gently, taking my arm.

I pulled free and took a step towards the gates. "I think we should go in," I said.

Freya shook her head. "That's a bad idea, Ivy," she said.

"I know, but I want to," I replied. "Just to look. To make sure."

"Make sure of what?" Freya said. "The police told us they'd found no sign of Conrad O'Connell or Dagmar Nilsson, or any of the Ash Tree Foundation people in there. It's like they vanished into thin air."

"Ivy doesn't mean that," Ruby said in a quiet voice that was so different to how she normally spoke. "She means make sure it was real. Right, Ivy?"

I stared at Ruby, then I nodded. That was exactly what I'd meant.

"Sometimes it feels like a dream," I said. "Sometimes I still dream about it."

"Ivy ..." Freya began, but Ruby interrupted her.

"It won't hurt to go in for a minute," Ruby said. "It might help to lay the ghosts to rest."

"I don't like this," Freya said. She pulled out her phone. "But if we're doing it, we'd better turn our locations off. I don't want Ella and my mum to freak out if they check on me and see I'm here."

I smiled at her. "Good thinking," I said. I pulled my own phone from my jeans pocket and switched the location tracker off.

At my side, Ruby was doing the same.

"All done," she said, putting her phone back into her bag.

"Let's get this over with," Freya said.

Ruby grabbed my left hand, and Freya took the right one.

Hand in hand, we slipped between the gates and started down the track towards the main building.

The track was overgrown, brambles tugging at my jeans as we walked. The trees along the pathway made it darker and colder than out on the street, and I shivered.

"We can still turn around," Freya said softly, but I shook my head and kept walking.

The track opened out into the grounds, and Chalmers Hall was right in front of us.

We clearly weren't the first people to come here since the Ash Tree Foundation had abandoned it. The walls were covered in graffiti, there were empty beer bottles on the ground and some of the windows had been smashed.

"Looks like it's become the local party spot," Ruby said. "The front door's open."

"No," Freya said. "We're not going inside."

I slipped my hands free of Ruby's and Freya's, and marched to the door.

Then I was inside Chalmers Hall once more.

I stopped in the hallway, remembering the last time I was here. I'd had to be carried outside by the police because I was too weak to walk after what the Foundation had done to me. I remembered how Conrad had attacked me in the ballroom after he'd tried to convince me to join them. He'd even tried to kiss me.

"I bet the whole place has been trashed," Ruby said, arriving at my side. Her voice echoed off the walls, and I looked around, seeing the broken furniture, the empty cans and crisp packets littering the floor. "And looted too. Some of the stuff in here was probably really valuable."

As Ruby wandered into Dagmar's old office, I pictured the vase I'd thrown at Conrad when I'd been trying to escape. It had been one of a pair that looked expensive – I'd thought that the first time I saw them.

"It's so weird to think we stayed here," Freya said, rubbing her arms as if she was cold. "Slept here. It feels really different now. I wonder if the attic has been looted too? Not that there was much in there to take."

I could hear Ruby opening and closing drawers inside Dagmar's office.

"You never did see the Blue Room, did you?" I asked. "The bedroom where Dagmar put me instead of the attic with you and the others. It was really nice." Despite everything, I hoped it hadn't been wrecked.

Freya shook her head.

"Come on. I'll show you. We'll be quick," I added. "Ruby, we're going upstairs."

"Obviously I'm coming," Ruby replied, bustling out of the office. "But look what I found duct-taped to the underneath of the desk."

She held up a huge brass ring with lots of keys hanging off it.

"I wonder why the police didn't find them?" Freya said, staring at the keys as if they might explode. "Taped under a desk isn't exactly a genius hiding place."

"Unless they were put there more recently – after the search?" Ruby suggested.

We all looked at each other.

"Maybe we should leave?" Freya said.

I stared at the keys Ruby was still holding up.

"Let's vote on it. I say stay," I said, surprising myself. But I'd come this far – I didn't want to turn around and leave. I wanted to put the Ash Tree Foundation and Chalmers Hall behind me for good. If I left now, this place would always haunt me. I wanted to be free of it, once and for all.

I continued, "Besides, if someone hid the keys there, it means they're not using them right now – it wouldn't make sense to hide them if they were here. So we should be safe."

"I agree," Ruby said. "And I want to see behind the scenes. Freya? What do you think?"

"I guess we're staying," Freya sighed. "But please let's be really careful. I don't like this."

"Of course. Do you think the keys are for here?" Ruby asked. "Or the weird folly in the grounds?"

"Here," I said. "The folly was all done with electronics and keypads. Everything was the latest tech."

I had a fleeting moment of longing for the Novo Reality headset I'd used down there. I pushed it aside.

My feet found their way back to the Blue Room easily, but the door wouldn't open. I rattled the handle and pushed against it in case the wood had swollen and made it stick, but it stayed closed.

"It's locked," I said.

We all looked at the ring of keys in Ruby's hand.

"Lucky we found them," Freya murmured as Ruby held the keys out to me.

It took me a few tries, but I found the right key and let us in.

The clock that used to be on the bedside table was gone, but otherwise the room looked the same as the last time I'd seen it. The bedcovers were thrown back just as I'd left them. There was even still a dent in the pillow from my head.

"OK, I can see why Dagmar was able to suck you into her creepy tech cult," Ruby said, staring around the room. "This place is unreal – it's like a film set. Four-poster bed, fancy dressing table, velvet curtains. Wait, does that bath have little lion feet?"

Ruby and Freya dashed into the bathroom, and I listened as they squealed about the claw-footed bathtub and how soft the towels were and how nice the soap was. I was surprised it was all still there – that no one had stolen it.

"And this bathrobe? It's the softest thing I've ever touched. Is it made of angels' eyelashes or something?" Ruby said. "It smells amazing too. Like fancy cologne."

I slipped the ring of keys into my pocket and crossed to the window. I looked out onto the grounds, just as I did the first time I was here. It was getting dark now – night was falling.

And then I saw a light heading towards the house.

CHAPTER 2

I darted to the bathroom.

"There's someone outside with a torch," I hissed.

Instantly, Ruby and Freya stopped talking, their eyes wide with horror.

"A security guard?" Freya whispered.

Ruby shook her head. "If they had security guards, the main doors would be locked. So would the gate."

My blood ran cold. "We have to get out of here," I gasped. "Follow me. Stay quiet."

I led them out of the Blue Room, along the upper landing to the big sweeping staircase. I paused at the top, listening.

The lower floor was silent.

On tiptoes, I started to creep down the stairs, staying close to the edges where they would be less creaky. I motioned for Freya and Ruby to do the same. I kept a watch for the light, listening hard for any sound, but there was nothing. I wished I had a weapon, a vase, *anything* to defend myself against whoever was there.

Finally, we reached the bottom of the stairs. The hallway was empty. Carefully, slowly, we headed for the door.

I held up my hand, signalling for Ruby and Freya to wait while I peeked out.

The coast was clear.

"Run for the gates on three," I said under my breath. "Don't stop until we're out. One ... Two ... Three!"

We burst from the door and streaked across the grounds. Ruby was in front, me in the middle and Freya just a little behind.

We reached the track, and I risked looking back, but no one was following us. Still, I kept running, following Ruby out of the gates and onto the main pathway. Our legs pumped until we reached where the houses began.

I crashed into Ruby, and Freya slammed into me. The three of us held each other, panting. There was a stitch in my side, and I pressed my hand against it, waiting for my heart to stop racing and my breathing to slow down.

"I really wish I hadn't eaten all that ice cream," Ruby said finally, holding her stomach. "My body isn't built to move like that."

"Are you sure you saw a light?" Freya asked me, turning to walk towards her house.

I fell into step beside her. "I'm positive."

"It was probably just the graffiti artists coming back to do another tag or something," Ruby said. She joined us on Freya's other side. "Or kids partying."

"Probably," I said, but I couldn't make myself believe it.

We didn't speak again during the walk back to Freya's. I felt terrible for ruining Freya's last night here, first by making her go into Chalmers Hall and then by making her run away from it.

"You're still coming for breakfast tomorrow?" Freya asked us when we stopped outside her front gate. "To say goodbye?"

"Absolutely," Ruby and I said.

"I'm—" I began, but Freya cut me off before I could say sorry.

"Don't apologise," she said. "It's fine. It's definitely been a memorable last night at home."

Freya grinned and I nodded, tears pricking my eyes. The three of us hugged goodnight.

As Freya went inside, Ruby set off towards her house and I turned for mine. I pulled out my phone and turned the location tracker back on. There were no messages – my mothers hadn't noticed what I'd done. As I walked, I tried to tell myself Ruby was right – the light was just other kids come to loot or graffiti or whatever. Or maybe it was some urban explorer looking for photos for their blog. But I couldn't stop it from bothering me. My skin felt itchy on the inside, like something was trying to get my attention.

I was almost home when it hit me.

The door to the Blue Room had been locked.

And I hadn't had a dressing gown when I'd been at Chalmers Hall. I especially hadn't had one that smelled of cologne.

I saw the Blue Room again in my mind: the thrown-back covers, the dent in the pillow where a head would fit. Surely it couldn't still be like that from when I'd been there? The police would have trashed the room when they searched it. But it didn't look messed up in that way. It looked like someone was living there. *Hiding* there. I felt the ring of keys in my pocket grow heavy.

What if whoever had the light was the same person who'd hidden the keys? What if they were the person who was hiding at Chalmers Hall?

What if it was Conrad O'Connell, returned to the scene of the crime a year later?

*

I tossed and turned all night. When I did manage to sleep, I had nightmares of Conrad O'Connell chasing me through Chalmers Hall, down corridors that went on for ever. In the dreams, I heard the jingling of keys like a bell as he ran after me, getting closer and closer …

The jingling turned into the ringing of my alarm, forcing me out of the dream. I felt like a zombie, but I couldn't miss Freya's goodbye breakfast. I got up and dressed, slipping the ring of keys for Chalmers Hall into my pocket.

"Have fun," my parents said as I left the house.

I nodded silently, feeling the weight of the keys against my leg.

I was halfway to Freya's when I froze in the street. I knew what I had to do.

I had to take the keys back to Chalmers Hall. I needed to put them back under the desk where Ruby had found them. If I did that, maybe we could pretend everything was fine. We could forget we'd returned and leave whoever was there to their peace.

If I hurried, I'd still make the breakfast on time.

When I got to Chalmers Hall, I slipped inside the gates and headed along the track, making myself move fast so I wouldn't have time to get scared or turn around.

The hall looked as abandoned as it had the night before, the broken windows like eyes staring back at me. It was chilly despite the sun, and I blamed that for the way I shivered as I looked at the house.

Once inside, I walked on tiptoes over to Dagmar's office.

I listened carefully, but I couldn't hear anything.

As silently as I could, I reached under the desk, searching. At last I found the edge of the tape that Ruby must have peeled away to release the keys, but something brushed my hand as it fell to the floor.

Frowning, I felt around until I found it and pulled it out.

It was a postcard with a picture of an animal skull on the front.

On the back was a message – "IT'S NOT OVER YET" – written in thick black writing.

CHAPTER 3

I ran as fast as I could to Freya's, the postcard clutched in my hand.

I stuffed it in my pocket when Freya's stepdad answered the door and invited me in.

"Ivy! You made it!" he greeted me.

"Hi, Mr Dixon. Sorry I'm late," I panted.

"Not to worry. I think there's still some food left. Go on in," he said, moving so I could pass him.

I dropped into the seat beside Ruby at the dining table. "You're late," she hissed.

I was desperate to tell her and Freya about the postcard. But I couldn't when Freya's mum, stepdad and her stepsister, Ella, were all there, finishing off what had clearly been a mountain of French toast and bacon.

"We need to talk," I whispered to Ruby under my breath. "All three of us, before Freya leaves."

Ruby shot me a questioning look, then nodded.

I helped myself to the last piece of French toast, but my stomach felt like it was the size of a walnut, and I knew I'd never be able to eat it. Meanwhile, the postcard was burning a hole in my pocket.

When breakfast was over, I tried to pull Freya aside so me, her and Ruby could talk. But she was too busy hugging her mum and stepdad, and helping Ella put the last of her things in Ella's car.

Then Freya was leaving.

"I'm going to miss you so much!" Freya said as she threw her arms around me. "I'll message you and Ruby everything we see on the drive to Scotland."

"Listen," I said, muttering into her ear.

But Ella was standing right next to us, trying to get Freya into the car, and she interrupted me.

"We have to go, Frey," Ella said, her voice impatient. "It's a really long drive."

"All right!" Freya said, releasing me from the hug.

A moment later, Freya was in the passenger seat of the car and driving away, and her mum was crying. Mr Dixon put an arm around her and led her back into the house, leaving me and Ruby alone.

"Damn it," I said.

"What's going on?" Ruby asked me. "What did you need to talk to us about?"

"This." I fished the postcard out of my pocket. "I took the keys back to Chalmers Hall this morning – that's why I was late. I found this stuck under the desk where the tape was."

Ruby took the postcard from me and read it. "This wasn't there last night. I'd swear on my life. I had a good rummage after I found the keys, and there was nothing ..." Ruby trailed off, shaking her head.

I'd never seen Ruby lost for words before. She always had a joke or a comment or a comeback.

It scared me to see her with nothing to say.

"It's Conrad," I said, filling the silence. "It must have been him last night when I saw someone with the light. I bet he saw us running away, realised we'd taken the keys and left this note instead, in case we returned them."

"What makes you think it's Conrad?" Ruby asked. "And what does 'IT'S NOT OVER YET' mean?"

"I don't know what it means, but I know it's him from the skull on the front," I told her. "When he was trying to draw me into the Foundation, he left an animal skull as a sign for me to follow the path that led to the folly in Chalmers Hall where the secret lab was. I think the skull on the postcard is Conrad's way of telling me it's him."

"Creepy," Ruby said.

"I think he wants to talk to me. I think the postcard is a test to see if I'll run to the police or if I'll listen to him."

"No way," Ruby said. "There's no chance we are speaking to that creepazoid." She took a deep breath. "But I think we should do a stakeout."

"What?" I was so shocked my jaw dropped.

"We should do a stakeout," Ruby repeated. "We'll go back to Chalmers Hall tonight. I'll say I'm at yours, you'll say you're at mine, and we'll wait for him."

"You don't think we need to call the police?" I asked. "Or at least tell our parents?"

Ruby gave me a dark look. "If you believed we needed to call the police, you would have called them already. And if we tell our parents, they won't let us out of their sight, and I don't feel like being under house arrest when I haven't actually done anything to deserve it. Besides, I'm not suggesting we talk to Conrad, especially if that's what he wants. I think the best thing to do is hide and film him – if it is him – and give *that* to the police. Evidence. More than a postcard."

"All right," I nodded.

"And one of us better call Freya and fill her in about the postcard," Ruby added. "She'll be furious if we don't keep her in the loop."

"I'll do it when I get home," I promised.

"Meet me at seven thirty tonight at the bottom of Freya's street," Ruby said.

*

My mothers were waiting for me when I got home, both of them in the living room, their arms crossed, their expressions worried.

I panicked that they'd checked my location and realised I'd gone to Chalmers Hall. I was going to be grounded for life.

"Sit down, please?" my mom asked. She guided me to the sofa and pushed me gently until I sat down.

She sat on one side, and my mum sat on the other. They both took one of my hands, and I knew I wasn't in trouble – there was no tandem hand-holding when I was. But something was seriously wrong.

"What's going on?" I asked. My skin crawled as if someone was walking over my grave.

"We didn't know if maybe someone said something while you were at Freya's," Mum said.

"Said *what*?" I asked. "Mum, you're scaring me. Just tell me what's happened."

My mum squeezed my hand. "Dagmar Nilsson has been spotted on a yacht in Honduras. She's with some billionaire tech baron." Mum rolled her eyes.

"Where's Honduras?" I asked.

"Central America," my mom said, switching into teacher mode – she was the headmistress at Chalmers High School. "There's no formal extradition treaty between Honduras and the UK," Mom continued. "It means Dagmar is safe from arrest there. It's typical of someone like her to run and hide with billionaires where she can't be held to account for her crimes. It makes me sick—"

"But the good news is, she's really far away from here," my mum gently interrupted Mom. She gave my hand another squeeze. "So that's one less thing to worry about."

"Is Conrad with Dagmar?" I asked, my heart beating fast in my chest.

"He must be," my mum said. "The report didn't say for definite, but where else would he be?"

I swallowed, my stomach churning.

"Right," I managed to say. "Where else?"

*

I called Freya, who was still in the car, on the long drive to Edinburgh. I could hear Ella in the background singing along to music I didn't recognise. It sounded like they were having fun, and I knew I couldn't tell her about Dagmar or the postcard on the call. I'd have to put it in a message.

Once Freya and I hung up, I opened the chat and typed out what my mothers had said about Dagmar. Then I looked it up online to find some links to post. One of the news reports had a photo of a blonde woman standing on a yacht, wearing white. The photo was taken from far away, but I could tell it was Dagmar.

In a separate chat, Ruby messaged me: *Should we tell Freya about tonight? I can't decide what's best.*

I mulled it over for a moment.

Not yet, I typed. *She'll only worry, and she's supposed to be settling in to Ella's flat. We'll tell Freya when we know for sure.*

OK, Ruby replied. *See you at seven thirty for* Operation Stealth. *Dress accordingly.*

*

When I got to the bottom of Freya's street, I saw Ruby waiting under a lamppost. She was dressed completely in black and wearing sunglasses. She looked like a cat burglar. Or a spy.

"What are you wearing?" she asked me. Ruby pulled down her sunglasses to stare at my hoodie and shorts. Her lip curled with disgust. "Ivy, that outfit isn't *Operation Stealth*. We need to be under the radar here."

I was relieved to see the old, dramatic Ruby back, but I didn't say that out loud. Instead, I grinned at her and gave a shrug.

"This outfit is easy to run in," I replied.

"Come on," Ruby huffed, linking her arm with mine. "But if we get caught, know it was your fashion choices that led to our downfall."

*

We sneaked back into Chalmers Hall just after eight. By then it was dusk, and the shadows were getting long. It made me nervous about what might be hiding in them.

First, we checked Dagmar's office. I felt under the desk.

"Any new postcards?" Ruby whispered.

"No. Nothing. The keys are gone too," I said.

"So he's been back." Ruby sounded grim. "He might be here now. We'd better check the Blue Room."

Ruby wouldn't let us use the torches on our phones, despite the fact it was really dark on the stairs.

"We don't need torches. Your legs are glowing in the dark," Ruby hissed behind me as we climbed up to the second floor.

"They are not," I replied.

"They practically are," Ruby grumbled. "I can't believe you wore shorts on a stakeout. Which part of *Operation Stealth* didn't you get?"

When we reached the top of the stairs, Ruby grabbed my hand. Together we moved down the hall, heading back towards the Blue Room. The door was open, just like we'd left it the night before.

We paused outside, both of us tilting our heads to listen. I looked at Ruby – I could just about see her face in the gloom. She held up a hand, extending three fingers.

She curled one down, and then the second, and when she'd done the third, we both rushed into the Blue Room.

It was empty, but the curtains were drawn over the window. Someone had been in here.

A light flared next to me, making me jump. But it was only Ruby. She'd turned on the torch on her phone.

"I think we should pause *Operation Stealth* for a minute," she said.

I turned my phone torch on too.

"Any sign of him?" Ruby asked. She began to poke around the room, her torch beam sweeping over the furniture.

"The curtains were open last night," I said, then I looked around. "But nothing else looks different to yesterday."

Ruby hummed. "There has to be something. If he is living here, he must have supplies."

I nodded. "Let's look."

Ruby opened the wardrobe, and I started opening drawers. It reminded me of the first time I'd been in this room – how I'd done the same. And just like then, the drawers only contained dead spiders.

Then I looked under the bed.

A plastic box had been shoved against the wall, beneath the top of the bed. I got on my belly and pulled it out.

Ruby came over to me, and we opened the box.

It was full of crisps and cereal bars and energy drinks – the kinds of foods that would stay fresh for a long time if they weren't opened. Not just food either – there was deodorant, cologne, toilet paper and soap.

"I think we found his stash," Ruby said. "Now I owe you an apology. It looks like you were right. Conrad's living here."

"What do we do now?" I asked.

From the doorway, a voice said, "You let me explain."

CHAPTER 4

I swung my torch towards the door.

Conrad O'Connell stood there, his hands held up in the torch beam. He squinted into the light.

"You don't get to explain anything, you little creep," Ruby said fiercely. She stabbed at the screen of her phone with her finger. "You're going to jail. I'm calling the police. The second my phone stops being useless."

"Please," Conrad said, desperation in his voice. He turned to me. "Ivy, listen to me before you call the police."

"Don't listen to him," Ruby hissed at me. She came to stand between me and Conrad. "And you" – she pointed at Conrad – "don't even look at her. Ivy, *you* call the cops. I'll watch him so he doesn't run. And if he tries, I'll brain him."

"I'm not going to run," Conrad said. "I'm glad you came back. I *want* to talk to you. Just give me a chance to explain before you decide what to do."

I stared at Conrad. I'd always imagined it would be scary to see him again.

The last time I was in the same room as him, I'd thrown a vase at his head and he'd called me a bitch. He'd tried to hurt me – kill me maybe. But now, looking at him, I found I wasn't scared at all.

In fact, I felt sorry for him.

"Maybe it wouldn't hurt to hear him out," I said to Ruby, putting a hand on her arm.

"Ivy!" Ruby stared at me. "What are you doing? He was going to let them kill me and Freya. And you! Remember?"

"I know—"

Ruby interrupted me. "He left you a creepy postcard! 'IT'S NOT OVER YET.' He said that – he wrote that!"

"I know," I said again. "But look at him," I added.

We both stared at Conrad, and he glanced down, not able to meet our eyes.

He was much thinner than he'd been last year. I could see his collarbones above the neckline of his T-shirt. His cheekbones were sharper too, making him look like a hunted fox. His hair was longer, brushing the neckline of his shirt, and it looked dirty and uncared for. There was patchy stubble on his cheeks, and his jeans had a hole in the knee. He was wearing his walking shoes, but I could see the soles peeling away.

If I'd walked past him on the street, I might not have recognised him. Conrad didn't look like a rich, popular influencer any more. He looked like someone my mothers would offer money to and ask if he needed help. He looked like someone living on the last of their hope.

"What is it you want to say?" I asked him. "Before I call the police," I added.

Conrad lifted his head and looked at me.

"First, that I'm sorry for what I did to you," he said. "I really am, Ivy. I regret it every day."

"You're sorry that Dagmar ditched you," Ruby snapped before I could reply. "You're sorry that she's living it up on a yacht in Honduras, drinking champagne with billionaires. While you're here, living off crisps in an abandoned house."

"What did you just say?" Conrad asked, staring at Ruby.

"That you're living off crisps—"

"No. You said Dagmar was in Honduras on a yacht. How do you know that?"

"It was all over the news earlier," I said. "There were photos of her."

"I knew it," Conrad muttered to himself. "That's what I meant by 'IT'S NOT OVER YET'. She's trying to keep Ash Tree Enterprises going. The Foundation – Project C – was only part of it, you know that. If she's on a yacht with billionaires, it's because she's still hoping to finish Projects B and A. Dagmar wants them to give her money."

"But she's a wanted criminal," Ruby said. "What good will money do?"

Conrad laughed. "You have no idea, do you? If Dagmar has enough money, enough power, she'll get immunity from prosecution. People like my aunt don't get arrested or go to jail for their crimes. They make a donation to someone, and the charges go away. And afterwards, they go ahead and do what they wanted all along."

We were all silent as we understood the truth of what he was saying. He was right – this happened with rich and powerful people all the time. My mum even said that the wealthy didn't pay fines – instead, they paid fees that let them break laws. People like Dagmar didn't go to jail without a real fight.

"You'd better tell us everything," I said finally. "Then we'll decide what to do next."

Conrad walked over to the bed and sat on the edge, his hands resting on his knees.

"Dagmar has been planning and building Ash Tree Enterprises for years," Conrad began. "Even before she married my uncle. It's her lifelong dream. Her legacy. Honestly, I'm pretty sure Dagmar only married my uncle for his money and his connections in the tech world. She was using him."

I nodded. Conrad had told me last year how his uncle had sold his technology solutions business and had been drifting around doing nothing until he met Dagmar.

I sat on the floor in front of Conrad and leaned against the door to the bathroom. After a moment, Ruby sat next to me. I glanced down at her phone and saw she'd finally managed to dial 999, her finger hovering over the *call* button. She looked at me and gave a single nod.

But Conrad wasn't paying attention to Ruby. He was focused only on me.

"Remember when you were down in the lab under the folly, and we told you that you were part of Project C?" he asked.

"Novo Reality, you mean," I said. Then I shivered.

Conrad gave me a look full of sympathy before he continued. "Launching Novo Reality was only one part of Dagmar's plan. Her endgame is to embed Ash Tree Enterprises products in everyone's lives – in every single bit of them. You know how there are always people who don't use technology or won't download apps? Well, Dagmar's dream is to make life impossible for them if they don't. She wants one hundred per cent involvement. Every person on the planet engaged with Ash Tree Enterprises. Logged in. All the time."

Conrad paused and took a deep breath.

"Novo Reality focused on people's social lives. Capturing their spare time and keeping them inside the Novo Reality world. Project B is about capturing everything else."

"What do you mean by 'everything else'?" Ruby asked.

"Project B is neurotechnology, like Novo Reality. But the catch is, it works IN reality," Conrad replied. "It isn't a headset you can take on and off – it's *inside* your head, activated all the time. Dagmar calls it Novo Life. A chip inside your brain that uses what you think to communicate directly with anything that it's linked to."

"It reads your mind?" Ruby asked, looking horrified.

"That's what Novo Reality did too," I said. "But only if you wore the headset. And it only worked in the Novo Reality world."

"This is designed to work in the *real* world," Conrad said. "Actual reality. That's the point of it. It will allow your thoughts to talk directly to anything that they're compatible with or linked to. Novo Life is like smart devices, but controlled by your brainwaves instead of voice commands or a phone app. So if your Novo Life chip is linked to a Novo Life keyboard app, you'll be able to type on it with your mind. Or if the lock on your front door is Novo Life compatible, you can open the door without saying a word."

"Who would want that?" Ruby asked.

People like me, said a voice inside my head, and I instantly hated myself. But it was true. Thousands – no, millions – of people would sign up for it for the chance to navigate the world like a superhero, operating anything just by thinking about it.

Conrad gave me a look like he knew what I was thinking.

Then he continued. "Eventually, Dagmar's plan is for Novo Life to be everywhere. In everything. And that's Project A. Total domination. If she completes Project A, you wouldn't be able to do anything without a Novo Life chip in your head.

"It starts out with small things like opening doors or using an app with the chip in your head, but eventually you need it for everything. If you wanted to pay for something in a shop, you'd use your chip to authorise the payment, and it would take the money from your account. Or if you wanted to get on a plane, you'd connect to a scanner at the airport, and it would check if you had a ticket, verify your identity and if you were allowed to fly. Your driver's licence, education records, your CV, your medical history. Every single important record about you would be on one chip inside your head."

Something terrible occurred to me. "What if the chip got damaged in an accident or something?" I asked, my heart beating hard against my ribs. I felt sick. "Would you lose everything about yourself?"

But I already knew what Conrad was going to say, and that was what was making me feel so ill.

"No," Conrad said. "Because the data on your chip would all be backed up on a database. Owned by Ash Tree Enterprises. Owned by Dagmar. And only Dagmar."

"She'd have everything," I said, horror filling my voice. "She'd control the world."

"What if someone hacked the database?" Ruby asked. "Could they get to the chip in your head? Could they take it over?"

Her face was pale, and I remembered why we'd met at the Ash Tree Foundation. Someone had hacked Ruby's phone and tried to ruin her life.

"That's what makes it all so dangerous," Conrad said. "But Dagmar doesn't care. Not as long as she has control first."

CHAPTER 5

It should have sounded impossible, like something from a film. The idea that Dagmar Nilsson would be able to control everyone in the world using chips in their heads.

But it wasn't much sillier than the idea that you'd be able to open doors and buy things in shops with a chip in your head.

Because *that* wasn't much sillier than being able to turn on all the lights in your house with an app, or have your fridge tell you what things you were running out of. Ten years ago, it might have been science fiction, but now it was real life.

And I'd met Dagmar. I'd been inside Novo Reality. I knew everything else that Ash Tree Enterprises had done to Ruby and to Freya and to so many other people with their products. The impossible was possible.

"It can't happen," Ruby said. "It's not right that one person could have that much power. No one will let this happen. The government …" Ruby trailed off.

"The government won't care if they make money out of it," Conrad said. "If Dagmar promises to open factories here to manufacture parts, or to host some of her servers here, or sell them exclusive contracts … They won't see the real danger – they'll just see the cash. You know that."

For a moment, none of us could speak as the truth sank in.

"We have to stop Dagmar before any of this happens," I said finally.

"And how do we do that?" Conrad asked. "She's not even in the country. She's in Honduras, hanging out with billionaires. It's only a matter of time before she convinces one of them to help her. If she hasn't already. And then she really will be untouchable."

"What if she *was* in the country?" Ruby said.

Her voice sounded brittle, but when I peered at her, there was a hard glint in her eyes. I knew that look – Ruby had an idea.

"Dagmar's not going to come anywhere near here," Conrad replied.

"Unless we convince her there's something here worth the risk of returning for," Ruby said. "Like, I don't know. Someone beating her to Novo Life and her plans to become a supervillain?"

Conrad laughed. "And who's going to do that?"

But I understood what Ruby was saying.

"Wait. No one actually has to do it," I said. "Dagmar just needs to *think* it's happening. That someone has stolen her big idea and is going to launch it before her. She knows you're still here, doesn't she?"

Conrad swallowed and nodded. "She abandoned me here. Where else could I go?"

"Exactly," Ruby said. "So you'd have every reason to turn traitor and want revenge then, wouldn't you?" She looked at me and smiled.

I grinned back at her. Then I turned to Conrad. "What if we can make Dagmar think that you went to one of her competitors and told them everything you know? It's been months since she ran away – that's enough time for someone else to have developed something like Novo Life, right, with your help and what you know? Maybe a new start-up company has developed a chip that works by using brainwaves to control something, and they're getting ready to launch it."

Conrad looked back and forth between me and Ruby, his face brightening as he understood what we were saying.

"Dagmar would be furious," he said. "Furious enough to come back to stop us."

"And if we can get her back here *before* she's all-powerful," I said, "she might actually get arrested."

Conrad's grin faded. "How do we do it?"

"With a lot of help," Ruby said. "Starting with Freya. Who YOU owe a massive apology to." Ruby pointed a finger at Conrad. "Let's call her now."

*

Freya didn't answer our call. Instead, she sent back a message that she'd only just arrived at the new flat and they were going straight out for dinner.

"Doesn't Ella's Margot work in tech?" Ruby asked me as she put her phone away. "Maybe she can help too. But we probably shouldn't tell her what we're doing. I can't imagine Ella will be on board with it."

"We'll talk to Freya tomorrow," I replied, seeing the time on my phone. "It's half past nine. My curfew's at ten."

"Mine too," Ruby said. "We'd better run."

"You're leaving?" Conrad asked.

"We'll be back tomorrow," I said, looking at Ruby. She nodded.

"OK. Hey ..." Conrad began and then stopped. "Never mind."

"What?" I asked. "What is it?"

Conrad was quiet for a long moment. Then finally he spoke. "I know I don't have the right to ask you for anything, but do you think you could bring me some food? I don't care what, so long as it's not crisps or cereal bars. And if you can't, that's totally fine."

"I'll see what I can do," I said. Ruby rolled her eyes at me. "Do you need anything else?" I asked. "Other than food. Toothpaste?"

Conrad blushed. "Clean socks would be great. Don't get new ones or anything. Just some old ones you don't wear any more would work."

"All right. Food and clean socks," I repeated.

Ruby rolled her eyes again and grabbed my arm.

"Let's go before our parents start to send out search parties," she said, pulling me away.

"Thank you," Conrad called from behind us.

As soon as we were out of Chalmers Hall, we started to run. I looked behind me just before we entered the wooded path to the main road. Conrad was watching us out of the window. He raised a hand to wave, and I quickly waved back.

"He has some cheek asking you to bring him food and socks," Ruby panted as we jogged down the street towards our part of town.

"It's not like he can ask anyone else, is it?" I wheezed back. I was getting a stitch.

"Even so," Ruby replied, puffing out her cheeks. "Do you really think we can pull this off?" she said a moment later.

"I don't think we have a choice," I said. "If we don't, then Dagmar will take over the whole world. Besides, we don't have to make a chip that does anything or launch it. Just make Dagmar think it's happening."

We slowed down at the top of the high street, where we'd split up.

"Listen, I think you should come to mine tomorrow morning," Ruby said. "We'll call Freya, just the two of us." She put her hands on her hips as she tried to catch her breath. "Now I think about it, I'm glad she didn't answer the phone and see us with Conrad. We should find out what she wants to do before we decide anything."

"But—"

Ruby cut me off. "I know you want to stop Dagmar. Out of all three of us she's hurt you the most. But everything that happened with AdelAIDE really messed Freya up—"

"I know that!"

"And the point of Freya deciding to go to university in Scotland was to start a new life, away from everything that happened here with Kim Hye-jin and AdelAIDE and the Ash Tree

Foundation," Ruby continued, holding up a hand so I'd let her finish. "She might not want to be involved in taking Dagmar down, and we have to respect that."

I knew Ruby was right. Freya had hated all the attention from the media after the truth about what was happening at Chalmers Hall came out. It had been really bad for me but even worse for Freya. The newspapers had dragged up everything that had happened with her and AdelAIDE all over again.

"All right," I said. "But we're still going to try to stop Dagmar, right?"

"Oh, *hell yes*," Ruby said, looking fierce. "I owe her. And if Freya does want to stay out of things, then I'll get Dagmar for Freya too."

*

"I'm in," Freya said.

I was in the kitchen at Ruby's house. Ruby's phone was propped up against a fruit bowl in front of us. I'd barely slept all night, wondering what Freya would say. I was scared that she would decide to stay out of it, scared she might even try to talk us out of it. But I needn't have worried. Freya hadn't hesitated as she declared she wanted to help.

"Are you sure?" I asked Freya. "If it works, it'll be all over the news again. *We'll* be all over the news again."

Freya nodded so fast the image on the phone screen blurred.

"I won't care if it means Dagmar's in prison and she can't do to anyone else what she's done to us," she insisted. "Let's do it. What's the plan so far?"

"Great question," Ruby said. "We don't have one yet."

"Don't worry. I have some ideas," Freya said. "Get a notebook and pen."

CHAPTER 6

Two hours later, Ruby and I were back at Chalmers Hall. This time we'd told our parents we were going to the cinema as cover. It meant that if they checked our locations, they'd think we'd turned our phones off during the film.

I was sitting opposite Conrad O'Connell, telling him Freya's plan while he ate the leftover buffet food we'd brought from Ruby's house. Her mum was a caterer, so the fridge was always stuffed with food she brought home after events.

"So ... the first thing that's going to happen is you'll reactivate your social media channels," I said. "You're going to make a video about how sorry you are for what you did with the Ash Tree Foundation and everything."

Conrad paused, a mini sausage roll halfway to his mouth. "OK," he said.

"You're going to say that you plan to hand yourself in to the police," I continued. "But first you want to make up for what you've done. And that's why you've been working with AltroWeb."

"What's AltroWeb?" Conrad asked.

"It's the fake company we made up," Ruby replied. "But as far as Dagmar is concerned, AltroWeb is all about a new way of being online. Specifically, by using a chip inside a person to control things. We're going to make it sound just like Novo Life. We want Dagmar to think AltroWeb were already working on a chip, but it was going slowly until *you* came along and told them everything you know."

"Gotcha," Conrad said, and ate the sausage roll in one bite. "Dagmar will really hate that," he added once he'd swallowed.

"That's the idea," Ruby said. "I'll be scripting and directing everything. Freya's going to pretend to her sister's girlfriend she wants to learn how to build a website and ask her how to do it, then set it up for us."

"Freya's going to deal with the social media accounts too," I added. "She's going to reactivate some of her old ones and strip all the content out to make it look like AltroWeb has been there for a while but just hasn't posted much yet."

"That's smart," Conrad said. "A lot of tech companies are really secretive, but if they appear completely out of the blue, it'll be suspicious. If Dagmar thinks it's just that she missed it because her attention was elsewhere, it'll feel more real."

"I'm going to ask some of the people from my performing arts group if they'll pretend to be AltroWeb employees for photos," Ruby continued. "And maybe do some videos too. They can use them for their showreels when they have auditions for other things."

"Basically," I added, "the idea is we convince Dagmar that AltroWeb has decided to launch the company because they're looking for investors. They've kept it quiet while they developed the technology, but thanks to your help it now works, meaning they're ready to go public and get the cash rolling in. We're going to pretend there's an exclusive, invite-only launch event that will include a demonstration of the chip working. We hope Dagmar won't be able to resist coming to see for herself. And then – *boom*. We'll call the police to the location of the fake launch, they'll find Dagmar there and arrest her."

"All right," Conrad said, reaching for a samosa. "So you're not going to do a real launch?"

I laughed. "How would we do that? Besides, we kind of need to keep this a secret from our parents. They'd notice if we were arranging a massive party."

"Of course, they'll find out when the trap is sprung and Dagmar is sent to jail," Ruby said. "But by then it'll be too late to stop us, and we'll be heroes. Ready to sell the rights to our life stories to Hollywood. And obviously I'll be playing myself."

Conrad looked at me, and we both bit back smiles.

"When were you thinking the launch would be?" Conrad asked, clearing his throat. "The fake launch, I mean."

"We haven't decided yet."

Conrad nodded. "Go for September 1st," he said. "It's Dagmar's birthday. It'll make her twice as angry."

"That's only a few weeks away," Ruby said.

"Tech moves fast," Conrad said.

"I'd better tell Freya," I said. I pulled out my phone and opened the group chat between me, Freya and Ruby. "Oh wow. Talking of fast, it looks like Freya's already done the website."

I clicked the link Freya had left in the chat. Opposite me, Ruby had pulled out her phone and opened it too.

"How did Freya do this in, like, two hours?" Ruby said.

Conrad leaned close to me to look at the website on my phone.

The website was simple and clean. The background was a pale, calm blue, with a dark blue border all the way around it. At the top of the page, in the centre, was the logo: a stylised spiderweb in dark blue, the edges softened so it almost looked like a target. It had an eye in the middle, sitting where a spider might. It rotated gently, waxing and waning like a moon. On its right, *AltroWeb* was written in a rounded font that matched the look of the logo. *Coming soon …* it said below.

Then there were tabs for *Founders*, *Aims*, *Frequently Asked Questions* and *Launch*. We clicked on all of them. There were no photos yet, or even any text, just the gently spinning logo, but it was there. It existed.

It had started.

"I guess it's too late to change our minds," Ruby said, expressing what I'd been thinking. "Which means I have scripts to write. Conrad, I need you ready for filming tomorrow." She looked him up and down and then turned to me. "I don't suppose you know how to cut hair?" Ruby asked.

"No. But there must be loads of haircutting tutorials online," I replied. "I'll figure it out."

"OK. And while you do that, I'll start writing."

Ruby started pacing, muttering to herself and making notes on her phone. Conrad looked at me, and I shrugged – this was clearly her writing process.

"Why don't you see if you can find some scissors?" I said to Conrad. He nodded, leaving me with Ruby.

I listened out until his footsteps had faded, then waved to get Ruby's attention.

"Do you really think we can trust him?" I asked in a low voice.

Ruby stared at me, her mouth open. "You were the one who said we should hear him out in the first place!"

"I know, but that's different to actually working with him. Can we trust him not to betray us?"

Ruby looked serious. "I'm not sure we have a choice. Conrad knows the plan. If he's not really with us, or if he uses this to run back to Dagmar, we'll soon find out. I hate myself for sticking up for him, but I think he really does want to stop her and make up for what he's done."

I hoped Ruby was right.

Conrad returned with a pair of scissors he'd found in Dagmar's office. He and I went into the Blue Room's bathroom.

"You need to wet your hair," I told Conrad, looking up at him from the haircutting video I'd been watching. "But I think I know what I'm doing."

He used the detachable showerhead to wet his hair, then sat on the side of the bath, his bare feet inside it, and I stood behind him.

It was so weird to be touching Conrad, to be combing his hair, and I thought it made him feel weird too. His breathing had gone funny, like he was trying to hold it or breathe quietly. I opened the music app on my phone and chose a playlist, putting it on so we didn't have to talk.

Then I cut Conrad O'Connell's hair.

I did it a little at a time, stopping every now and then to go back to the video. When it was time to do the front, I made Conrad turn around. I was grateful his eyes were closed.

"What are you going to do once Dagmar's been arrested?" I asked him.

"Hand myself in," Conrad said.

"Really?"

Conrad opened his eyes. "Really. I deserve to be punished for my part in it. For what I did to you."

"I thought you were going to kill me," I said quietly.

"No!" Conrad said, his voice echoing in the tiled bathroom.

"Everything OK?" Ruby called from the bedroom. A second later, she appeared in the doorway.

"Fine," Conrad and I said at the same time.

Ruby looked at us with suspicion, her eyes narrowed, then she disappeared back into the Blue Room.

"No," Conrad said again. "I never would have. Never, Ivy."

"You called me a bitch," I reminded him. "You were really angry."

"You had just thrown a vase at my head," Conrad said. "But I wouldn't have hurt you," he added. "I was just going to grab your hands so you couldn't throw anything else. I swear it."

We both looked at the scissors gripped in my hand.

"All right," I said after a long moment. "Close your eyes while I do the front."

Conrad shut them.

"Done," I told him a few minutes later.

I stepped back as he stood up and looked in the mirror. Conrad frowned at himself, pulling at his hair and then mussing it up.

Without saying a word, he left the bathroom. My stomach dropped – had I done it wrong? Did he hate it?

He came back with a bundle of cloth and a washbag.

"Give me a second?" he asked, and I nodded.

"OK."

I went back out into the bedroom, where Ruby was typing frantically on her phone.

"Almost done," she muttered.

I started to pace, suddenly anxious.

"Finished!" Ruby declared a few moments later, just as the bathroom door opened and Conrad walked out.

He'd changed into a less tatty T-shirt and clean jeans, and he'd done something with his hair – put some product in it or something.

He looked almost like Conrad O'Connell, famous influencer, again.

"Right on time," Ruby said, handing him her phone. "Here are your lines."

Conrad scrolled the screen, nodding to himself. Then he took a deep breath and raised his head, looking directly at me like I was the camera of his phone.

"Well, hi there. Long time no see," he said. His mouth spread into a wide smile. "I'm Conrad O'Connell. Did you miss me?"

CHAPTER 7

I was at home when Ruby posted the video. We'd filmed the whole thing right after I'd cut Conrad's hair. Then Ruby had made him hand over his login details so she could post it when the time was right.

I saw the notification pop up on my screen from Ruby saying "WE'RE LIVE!" while I was in the middle of making food to take to Conrad.

I was almost finished spooning mayonnaise into cold pasta, leftover roast chicken and red peppers when my mum came into the kitchen.

"Ivy?" she said.

I hummed in reply, stirring the food.

"Ivy, look at me a second," my mum insisted.

There was an edge to her voice, and I turned round, the spoon in my hand. Her expression was serious.

"What's wrong?" I asked, suddenly worried someone had died or that we were moving house.

"Conrad O'Connell has posted a video online."

"Oh my god," I said, almost dropping the spoon with relief.

My mum mistook my relief for panic and strode over to me, taking my arms.

"It's going to be OK," she said firmly, shaking me to emphasise it. A blob of mayonnaise fell to the floor. "I'm sure the police are already looking for him. I'm sure they have ways of finding out where it was filmed, and they're probably already on their way to arrest him."

I really hoped not.

"What was the video about?" I asked, turning back to the pasta in case my face looked suspicious. "Wait." I spun around again to face her. "How do you know he's posted a video?"

To my surprise, my mum blushed.

"I ... started following him after everything that happened," she said in a rush. "Just in case he posted anything about you. I didn't want to wait to find out from the news. To be honest, I'd forgotten I'd done it until his video came up in my feed." Mum paused. "Do you want to watch it together?"

I'd already seen it twice, both live as Conrad filmed it and afterwards when he'd edited it, so there was nothing in it that could surprise me.

"Sure," I said.

My mum pulled her phone from her jeans pocket and unlocked it, propping it up against the pasta bowl. There he was – Conrad O'Connell, his hair freshly cut by me, standing against a plain white wall that wouldn't reveal anything about his location.

"Ready?" my mum asked.

When I nodded, she pressed play.

"Well, hi there. Long time no see," Conrad said from the phone. "I'm Conrad O'Connell. Did you miss me? I know you've probably been wondering where I am and what I've been doing, and I know a lot of you are really, *really* disappointed in me. And I don't blame you. I'm here today to apologise for my part in what happened at the Ash Tree Foundation, and for lying to you all about my involvement with technology. I have let down everyone who ever trusted me and believed in me, and for that I'm truly sorry.

"I built my brand based on living a reduced-tech life, and I should have stuck with that. I shouldn't have listened to my aunt when she invited me to join her company. I should have followed my gut and said no. But instead, I let Dagmar Nilsson convince me that her approach to technology was different. I believed her. I trusted her. And because I did, I made some terrible mistakes, and I've been part of something that's hurt a lot of people. Including someone I really cared about."

In my kitchen, I froze.

I'd asked Ruby to cut this part because when Conrad had filmed it, he'd looked beyond the camera straight at me. I could see him doing it on my mum's phone screen – his eyes lifting for just a second to where I'd been standing. Like he was talking to me.

I glanced at my mum to see if she'd noticed, but she was still staring at her phone, shaking her head, her lips pursed.

"To that person, and to everyone, including all of my fans and followers, I really am so sorry,"

Conrad continued in the video. "And I want to make up for it. Actions speak louder than words, so I plan to hand myself in to the police very soon, to tell them everything I know about my aunt's activities. But before that, I have some news.

"I've been working with a company called AltroWeb. Like my aunt, they're working hard to develop new technology, but unlike Dagmar Nilsson, they don't want to hurt or use anyone. They truly want to make the world a better place, and I still want that too. That hasn't changed. So I've told them everything I know about the Ash Tree Foundation and its plans, and they've used that information to create something incredible. That's all I'm allowed to say for now, but you'll be hearing a lot more about us soon. In the meantime, go to altroweb.com for more information."

The video ended.

At my side, my mum snatched up her phone and shoved it back in her pocket as if she was afraid Conrad O'Connell would climb out of it.

"How are you feeling?" she asked me. "Talk to me."

"I don't know what I'm feeling," I said. "What do you think?"

My mum snorted. "Well, I don't believe it for a second. All that 'I believed her too' nonsense, making out he's a victim here."

"Right," I said.

I went over to the cupboard where the plastic containers lived and pulled one out.

"What's that for? You can just put the bowl in the fridge with a cover on if you're not eating it now."

"I'm taking it out with me," I replied.

My mum stilled. "You're going out?" she asked.

Sensing danger, I nodded and began to spoon the pasta salad into the plastic container. "I said I'd meet Ruby. We're going 'location scouting', whatever that means." I tried to make my voice casual.

"Do you think that's a good idea?" my mum asked. "With Conrad on the loose again?"

"He's always been on the loose," I said. My cheeks were burning.

I kept my back to my mum as I continued. "And he's not going to be anywhere near here. Especially not after the video. This is the first place the police will look. He has no reason to be here without his aunt. Chalmers Hall was Dagmar's house. Not even *her* house – her husband owns it. Conrad's probably back in his home town."

This was me improvising on the spot. Ruby would have been proud of me.

"Or maybe he's on the yacht too," I said. "Maybe he's with Dagmar, and all this AltroWeb stuff is a distraction from her. It's a bit suspicious that a video of him comes out just a day after she's seen, don't you think? What did Mom say that tactic was called? Dead Cat Strategy? When someone makes a really shocking announcement or does something to distract you from the thing they don't want you to think about?"

I put the lid on the container of pasta and turned to my mum. To my relief, she was nodding.

"The timing is a little strange, now you mention it. Still," Mum said, "you're always out lately. When was the last time you played one of your games?"

I laughed – I couldn't help it.

"Seriously?" I grinned at my mum. "You want me to embrace the gamer life again? That's how I ended up at the Ash Tree Foundation in the first place, remember?"

"I know," she grumbled. "I didn't expect to say it either. But now I just think I preferred when you were upstairs, and I could keep an eye on you. I suppose you're right. You'd better hope your mom agrees when she gets back from work."

I crossed the kitchen to my mum and kissed her on the cheek. "You could always not tell her about the video."

My mum looked stern. "You know we don't keep secrets from each other," she replied. "And besides, this will be everywhere by tonight."

"Then I'd better make the most of my freedom," I said. "I'll see you later. Love you."

"Love you!" Mum called after me.

When I reached the bottom of my street, I pulled out my phone to tell Ruby I was on my way.

To my surprise, the group chat notification said I had thirty-two messages waiting. I opened the app.

One message from Freya caught my attention. It was written in capital letters with too many exclamation marks to count.

IVY, SHE REPLIED!!!!!!!!!!!!!

It seemed Dagmar Nilsson had already taken the bait.

CHAPTER 8

I turned my location off before I ran all the way to Chalmers Hall, the plastic container of pasta salad rattling under my arm.

Ruby was already there, sitting next to Conrad. She was talking into her phone, held up in front of them. I heard Freya's voice coming from the speaker.

A sharp pain twisted in my stomach when I realised they were talking to Freya without me. But I forced myself to take a deep breath. This was how Dagmar had got to me last year. She'd isolated me from my friends. I wouldn't let her do it again.

"What's happening?" I asked, making my way over to them.

Ruby scooted along to make space for me, and I sat beside her, clutching the box of food, my heart beating hard.

"Hey, Ives," Freya said, waving on the screen. "Thank god you're here."

Freya's words made me feel much better, and I waved back. "What did I miss?" I asked.

"We're trying to decide what to reply," Ruby informed me.

"First things first. How can we be sure it's Dagmar?" I said.

"Show her," Conrad said to Ruby.

Ruby lowered her phone, making Freya's face disappear as she opened the inbox on the video app.

Nice try, Conrad, the message began. *But we both know you were only ever useful as the face of the Ash Tree Foundation, not the brains.*

It *could* be Dagmar, I supposed. The account was clearly a burner, the username a jumble of random letters and numbers, with no profile picture. I reached out and opened the poster's profile. It was blank, with a blue *New* label at the top. But then again, it could be anyone.

Ruby toggled back to the inbox, and I saw there were hundreds of messages in there, most of them unread.

"Have you looked at any of the other messages?" I asked.

Conrad sighed. "We started, but a lot of them are just telling me to hand myself in to the police. Some tell me to die." He paused before continuing, "And the rest are from people—"

"Girls," Ruby interrupted him.

"—offering me a place to hide out," Conrad finished.

His cheeks had turned pink.

"We figured we should pay more attention to new or anonymous accounts," Conrad said. "Because Dagmar would probably use a burner. And it looks like she did."

Ruby swiped the screen so we could see Freya again.

"So … what should we say?" Ruby said.

"I think we should ask Dagmar to prove it's her," Freya replied. "What do you think, Ivy?"

I considered it for a moment. "I'm not sure. Maybe we should do nothing for now and let her stew," I said. "We'll make a new video in a few days and see if she bites again. If it's really her."

"It's definitely her," Ruby said. "But—" She was interrupted by her phone beeping in her hand. "Oh no. Call waiting. It's my mum. Freya, I have to go. I'll take it as a voice call. Don't speak," Ruby ordered Conrad as she ended the video call with Freya.

Ruby took a deep breath, cleared her throat and swiped left to accept her mum's call.

"Greetings, mother of mine," she crowed. "What is it?" Ruby's voice became higher. "Well, I didn't turn it off."

Ruby pulled a panicked face at me, and I understood what had happened. Mrs Brooks had checked Ruby's location and realised it was switched off.

"I'm at Ivy's," she said. "Ivy, inform my mother we're fine."

Ruby held the phone out towards me, and I bellowed, "Hi, Mrs Brooks. How are you?"

"Ivy, are your mothers home?" Mrs Brooks said.

"No. Mom's at work and my mum's gone to the shops," I told her.

"Do they know?" Mrs Brooks demanded.

I locked eyes with Ruby. "About?" I said carefully.

"That boy from the Foundation being back in the spotlight?"

"Oh. Yeah. Actually, my mum is the one who showed it to me," I said.

Ruby gaped at me, and I nodded to tell her it was true.

"Really? And what does she think about it?" Ruby's mum asked.

"Well …" I began.

Ruby waved her hand at me, urging me to come up with something.

"Dead Cat Strategy," I said, repeating the tactic that had worked on my own mum, twisting it to sound like she came up with it, not me. "You know, to distract us from Dagmar being on the yacht. It's probably that Conrad is there too and he's put out the video to make everyone forget about Dagmar."

We all held our breath.

"I suppose that would make sense," Mrs Brooks said slowly, just like my mum had. "Distraction techniques. Like politicians do. The timing *is* very convenient."

"That's exactly what Mum said. She reckons he'd have to be a fool to be anywhere near here," I added as Conrad grinned at me. "I don't think she's worried right now. I think she wants to wait and see what happens next."

Ruby began to bow to me. Conrad gave me a salute.

"OK, thanks, Ivy," Mrs Brooks said. "Put Ruby back on."

"I'm here, Mum," Ruby said, pressing the phone back against her ear. "Yes. I will. Yes. OK. I said yes. I love you too. Bye."

She ended the call and looked at me.

"I need to go," Ruby said. "I've got about ten minutes before she calls back to ask why I still haven't turned my location back on, and I need to be miles away from here when I do."

"But Ivy just got here," Conrad said. "You could stay, couldn't you?" He turned to me.

"Oh, thanks," Ruby huffed.

"No, I'd better go too," I said. "My mum really did show me the video, and she was pretty nervous. If she decides to check my location and it's off, she might not call me but call Ruby's mum instead, and then we're all done for."

Conrad's face fell. "Yeah, of course."

"But there's pasta here." I handed him the plastic container. "We'll try to come back tomorrow. I'll bring more food."

"And we can do another video. If anything major happens, we'll let you know," Ruby said.

"Yeah. OK," Conrad said. His voice was sad.

Ruby and I stood up. Conrad came too, walking us down the stairs and to the front door of Chalmers Hall.

"Will you be all right?" I asked him just before we left.

"Of course," Conrad said, smiling sadly. "See you."

"Bye."

I looked back at Chalmers Hall just before Ruby and I turned down the wood-lined track that would take us to the main gates.

Conrad was still standing in the doorway. He looked small and lonely. When I waved, he waved back, keeping his hand up until I couldn't see him any more.

It would be better for him if we could end this all soon. It would be better for all of us.

*

Ruby came back to my house with me. I put on some music in case my mum came up the stairs, and we called Freya back from my phone this time.

She was in her new bedroom in Scotland. Freya gave us a quick tour, then threw herself on top of the covers of her bed and propped her laptop against the pillows.

"Dagmar must have an alert on Conrad's channels, like your mum, Ivy," Freya said. "So she'd know as soon as he posted."

"So you really think it's her?" I asked.

"You asked that before," Ruby pointed out. "Does that mean you think it isn't?"

I shrugged. "I'm not sure. I wish we had a way of knowing for definite that it was Dagmar."

"I told you we should ask for proof," Freya said on the screen. "Like a selfie of her on the yacht. Or maybe we could ask her something only she would know. Ivy, did she ever say anything to you that we could use?"

I mulled it over for a moment, trying to remember what Dagmar and I had talked about.

"Possibly," I said. "The first time she spoke to me about Project C, she talked about symbiosis. I didn't know what it meant, so she told me. It's when two species develop a close and long-term relationship that helps them both survive. Maybe we could mention that somehow?"

"But if we did, she'd know you were involved," Freya pointed out.

"That might not be a bad thing," Ruby said. "After all, she says in the message that Conrad doesn't know enough to betray her, but Ivy actually used Novo Reality. She knows how it works. So perhaps we could convince Dagmar that Ivy and maybe a few of the other people who worked at the Ash Tree Foundation have teamed up with Conrad and gone over to AltroWeb. That might make her really interested."

"It's risky," Freya said. "And it puts Ivy back in the firing line. What do you think, Ives?"

"It might be worth it," I said. "I mean, if it's not Dagmar, then it won't matter. And if it is, we'll know for sure, and, like you said, it could scare her into doing something we can use. Let's do it."

"You're sure?" Ruby asked.

I pictured Conrad living rough at Chalmers Hall. How he'd said that when it was over, he'd hand himself in too because he deserved to be punished. How he'd said he was sorry.

Then I remembered Ruby's mum and my mothers, and how worried they still were about us. We'd never be truly safe or happy until this was properly finished. The sooner Dagmar was arrested, the sooner we could all get on with our lives for real.

"I think maybe I'd rather know for sure so we can end this."

Ruby nodded to agree, and on the phone screen, Freya did the same.

"All right," Ruby said. "Let me just think what to say to her ... How about: 'Maybe I didn't need to know exactly what you were doing. Maybe I just needed to build relationships with people who did. Do you know what symbiosis means?'"

A chill ran down my spine. "Yes," I said. "That's good. Rubes, that's brilliant."

"What about: 'DON'T you remember what symbiosis means?' instead?" Freya said. "It sounds a bit more threatening."

"Perfect," Ruby muttered, typing into her phone. "I still can't believe I'm logged into Conrad O'Connell's social media. This is wild." She read out the planned message again, and when Freya and I nodded, Ruby sent it.

"I wonder how long— Oh my god, she's typing!" Ruby said.

I looked and saw the three dots that told me Ruby was right. Whoever it was must have been waiting for us to reply.

"What time is it in Honduras?" I asked.

Freya leaned forward so we got a close-up of her chin. I heard the sound of typing coming from the speaker.

"It's ten twenty in the morning there. They're seven hours behind us."

"She's replied!" Ruby yelped.

So you managed to convince Ivy to help you? the message said. *Big mistake. Both of you will regret it.*

"It's her," I said, my blood turning cold. "It's really her."

CHAPTER 9

For a moment, we were all frozen. Then something took over my body, something hot and angry.

I took Ruby's phone from her.

Not just Ivy, I typed. *You treated a lot of people very badly. Left a lot of people behind. So who really made the big mistake?*

"Damn, Ivy, you don't want to make her too angry," Ruby said, pulling her phone from my hands.

"Angry people make silly mistakes," I said.

"They also lash out," Freya said on the phone. "And Dagmar's got a lot of rich and powerful friends."

"Yeah, in Honduras," I said. "Besides, we *want* her to come back. So if this is what it takes, so be it."

"She's replied again," Ruby said. *"Bringing you in was my biggest mistake,"* she read aloud.

"That's cold," Freya said.

I felt a pang of pity for Conrad.

"But it's one I can at least fix," Ruby said. "Dagmar just sent that too."

"Fix how?" Freya and I said at the same time.

Ruby typed it out, and we waited.

But this time Dagmar didn't reply.

"What do we do now?" Ruby asked. It had become clear that Dagmar was done speaking with us.

"We wait," Freya said. "When are you doing the next video?"

"Tomorrow," I said.

"We'll post it Thursday," Ruby added.

"Great. In the meantime, I'll add some stuff to the website."

"How did you do the website so fast?" I asked Freya. "I've been meaning to ask."

"Oh, it's easy. I didn't even need to ask Ella's Margot how. I looked it up online, and there were loads of website builders available, so I picked the one that looked the easiest. It basically does everything for you. Even with the logo – it generated it for me, and then I animated it to spin." On screen, Freya looked pleased with herself.

I heard someone knocking on a door in the background, then a voice speaking. Freya looked up over the screen of her laptop.

"That's Ella," she said. "We're going on some Ye Olde Scotland tourist tour. Talk later."

Then Freya was gone, the screen turning dark as she closed her laptop.

"Now what?" I asked Ruby.

"I'd better get home," Ruby said, rolling herself off my bed. "My mum's not working tonight. Maybe if I put in some mother-daughter time, it'll make her relax about Conrad being on the loose. I'll talk to you later."

When Ruby was gone, I tried to play one of my old *Legend of Zelda* games, but I couldn't concentrate, making silly mistakes. I smashed the buttons on the controller, trying to make

Link leap out of the way of a Black Hinox. But all I could think of was Dagmar's message: *But it's one I can at least fix.*

There was only one thing I could think of that she might mean. I'd been trying to ignore it all afternoon, but as the Hinox swiped its staff into Link and he collapsed to the ground, I couldn't think of anything else.

I needed to warn Conrad that his aunt was planning to kill him.

*

But I didn't get the chance. My mom came home and heard about the video, and she wouldn't let me go out again.

We were standing at the back of the living room, on either side of the dining table, glaring at each other. My mum had retreated into the kitchen to wash up after dinner, leaving me and Mom to fight it out.

"I promised Ruby I'd help her learn lines tonight," I lied. "And Conrad's not going to be anywhere near here," I added.

"You don't know that," my mom said. "The fact is, we don't know where he is, and until we do, I'd rather you stayed in at night."

"This is ridiculous," I yelled. "The only reason any of this even happened was because you sent me to the Ash Tree Foundation in the first place. You said you wanted me to have real friends and a life. Now I do, you're trying to take them away from me."

My mom turned pale. "No, Ivy, I'm not. I just …"

To my complete surprise, she sagged against the table.

"You're right," my mom said. I'd never heard her say that before. "It is our fault. If we hadn't sent you to that place, none of it would have happened, and I'm really sorry for that. If I could get my hands on that Dagmar woman …" Mom stopped and took a deep breath. "Listen, why don't you ask Ruby to come here instead? We can even go and pick her up and get dessert on the way back."

I couldn't think of what to say – Ruby couldn't come over even if that had been my real plan because she was spending time with her mum tonight.

"Fine. I'll ask her," I muttered furiously, pulling out my phone. I pretended to type a message and wait for a reply. "She can't. Ruby's mum wants her to stay in tonight," I said.

I realised too late I'd given my mom the exact ammunition she needed.

"Well, if Mrs Brooks is making Ruby stay home tonight," Mom said, "there's nothing stopping you staying in either. And it won't kill you to spend one night apart."

Maybe it wouldn't kill me, but it could kill Conrad.

But there was no point in arguing with my mom. She always won.

"Fine. I might as well go to bed then," I said.

And I really did, watching videos on my phone until I heard my mom double locking the front door downstairs.

After I'd come home from the Foundation, they'd always checked on me before they went to bed. As soon as I heard my mothers coming up the stairs, I shoved my phone under my pillow and pulled the covers right up so they couldn't see I was still dressed.

I was breathing slowly and evenly as they opened my bedroom door, like I was deeply asleep. I didn't move, not even after they closed the door. Instead, I waited while they brushed their teeth, murmuring to each other while my mum put her face cream on and my mom put her hair in a braid. I heard them go into their room. And then I waited some more, until I was sure they must be asleep.

I sneaked out of my room, my phone in my pocket, and checked there was no light under their door. Then I crept down the stairs, grabbed my trainers from the hall and tiptoed into the kitchen, opening the back door silently. I moved like a ghost down the garden path and climbed over the fence at the back onto the street.

And then I started running, heading for Chalmers Hall.

*

I arrived in record time, charging up the stairs to the Blue Room.

Conrad had locked the door, and I knocked on it urgently.

"Conrad, it's me!" I hissed, my knuckles rapping the wood. "Open up!"

A few seconds later, he did, blinking against the light from my phone's torch.

"We have to go," I said, pushing past him and into the room. "She's going to kill you."

"Who? Ivy, what are you doing here? What time is it? What's going on?"

"Dagmar," I began to explain. "Ruby and I messaged her again this afternoon."

"You what?" Conrad said.

"*Listen to me!* I came here to warn you. Dagmar said she was going to fix you, and I'm pretty sure she means—"

I stopped talking suddenly, my heart in my throat.

From beyond the room, down the stairs, I'd heard a noise.

"Ivy—" Conrad started.

I flew at him and clamped my hand over his mouth.

"I think someone's here," I whispered. "We have to go."

I grabbed his hand, pulling him from the room and along the corridor.

His grip tightened on mine as I heard another creak – the sound of someone at the very bottom of the stairs, someone who didn't know to use the edges to keep the steps from creaking.

Conrad jerked me to a stop. "This way." He said it so quietly I barely heard him.

I let him pull me down the corridor, away from the stairs and around a corner. My pulse raced so fast I felt sick. Conrad stopped at the very end of the passageway and let go of my hand, using both of his to push at the wall.

"Conrad, we don't have time …"

I fell silent in shock when the wall opened silently and Conrad urged me inside, pulling it closed after him. I'd had no idea anything like this was here.

It was pitch-black inside the wall, but Conrad took my hand and started walking slowly. I followed him until he stopped.

"Stairs coming up," he said. "Keep one hand on the wall as you walk. I'll be in front of you, and I'll count so you know when they're coming."

I edged forward carefully and found where the steps began, then I reached for the wall with my hand.

"One," Conrad said, and I took the first step.

Somewhere on the other side of the wall I could hear voices. My already speeding heart kicked up another gear.

If they found us here, we'd be sitting ducks.

But I kept going, kept walking, as Conrad whispered numbers back at me.

"Landing," Conrad warned me, and we crossed it. "There are more stairs. Ready? I'll start from one again. *One ... Two ... Three ... Four ...*"

I couldn't hear anything above us any more, only Conrad's numbers.

"*Five.* We're almost at the bottom. *Six.* We'll come out next to the kitchens. *Seven*," Conrad kept going.

"Where are we?" I asked, keeping my voice super-quiet.

"*Eight.* It's the servants' staircase. *Nine.* A lot of old houses – *ten* – had them so the people who lived there – *eleven* – wouldn't have to see the staff coming and going. *Twelve.* I found it when I explored the house – *thirteen* – after Dagmar and my uncle bought it."

"Does she know about it?" I asked him.

"*Fourteen.* I doubt she even knows where the kitchens are, let alone the servants' stairs. *Fifteen*," Conrad whispered back. "*Sixteen.* Dagmar only cared about the folly. *Seventeen.* OK, we're almost there. *Eighteen. Nineteen. Twenty.* That's the last one. And the door is just ... along ... here. Ready?"

"For what?" I asked as Conrad stopped walking.

"We're going to run. We can go out of the kitchens – someone broke the door off there. Then out into the grounds. We'd better avoid the front, but we can head into the woods and circle around. Do you remember anything from when we learned orienteering?" Conrad asked.

I shook my head, then remembered he couldn't see me and said, "No."

"OK. Then you're going to have to trust me," Conrad said. He sucked in a deep breath.

"What?" I asked.

"Thank you for coming to warn me," he said. "I know I don't deserve it."

"You don't deserve to be murdered."

"Still, thanks."

With that, Conrad opened the wall.

Moonlight streamed in from some skylights above, and I could see we were in a long, narrow passageway.

Ahead of us was a door, hanging off its hinges.

Conrad stopped just before it. "Head for the woods, keep left and it'll bring us back around," he said. "OK?"

I nodded.

"Run!"

We burst out into the gardens, and I realised it was the same part of the grounds onto which the Blue Room looked out.

It meant if anyone was in that room and they glanced out of the window ...

Something whizzed past me and struck the dirt with a thud. A split second later, I heard a loud crack.

"Ivy, they've got a gun!" Conrad screamed.

CHAPTER 10

My body took over, and I began to sprint as more shots rang out. It didn't feel real. I zigged and zagged like I was in a game, my legs pumping as fast as I could make them. I moved like lightning towards the trees, Conrad at my side.

Somehow we made it into the woods, into the cover of the trees, and the gunfire stopped.

"They're not shooting any more," I said to Conrad.

"Which means they're coming after us," Conrad replied. "We have to keep going. This way," he urged, turning right.

"You said left, towards the gates!" I reminded him.

"They probably came that way, and we don't know if there's anyone waiting. We'll go over the wall near the pond, straight onto the street. We'll be safer there. Hopefully."

From my pocket came the faint sound of my ringtone.

"Is that your phone?" Conrad asked.

"Yes," I gasped.

I'd completely forgotten I had it with me. A cold wave broke over me as I realised what would have happened if it had rung while we were in the servants' stairway.

There was no way to fish it out of my pocket while I ran, so I left it ringing, hoping the attackers were too far away to hear it. But as soon as it stopped, it started up again.

We reached the pond and ran around the edge, heading towards a wall.

I glanced behind us, but we were still alone. We'd be harder to track in the dark too.

"The main road is on the other side of the wall," Conrad said. "We'll have to climb it. Do you think you can?"

In response, I threw myself at the wall, my fingers gripping the top. With a strength I didn't know I had, I hauled myself up, using my toes to dig into the brick and push me upward.

Then I was on top and tipping over the other side, falling into the grass verge between the wall and the road.

Conrad landed next to me like a cat, bouncing straight to his feet.

"We have to keep going," he said, grabbing my arm and pulling me up. "We don't— No!" Conrad yelled as a pair of car headlights rounded the corner and landed on us. "Ivy, run!"

I started to sprint again as the car beeped its horn frantically.

At the same time, my phone began ringing again.

And then I heard my mum's voice. "Ivy! Ivy Finch, you stop right there!"

"Mum?" I said, whipping around.

My legs turned to jelly as I saw the car – our car – slowing down. My mum was leaning out of the passenger-side window.

I'd forgotten to turn my location off. They must have woken up, realised I'd gone out and come after me. I raced towards them.

"What the hell do you think you're playing at?" my mum screamed. "Get in this car, right now!"

She didn't have to tell me twice.

"This way," I shouted at Conrad, heading for the car. "Don't stop," I said to my mom as I ripped the back door open and threw myself inside.

A second later, Conrad followed, flinging himself into the backseat beside me and slamming the door behind him. Both of my mothers started screaming. My mom hit the brakes.

"No, don't stop! Drive!" I shouted. "Hurry!"

I saw a pair of hands appear on the top of the wall.

"Mom, they have a gun. Drive!" I said.

And to her credit, she did.

*

Half an hour later, my legs still felt like all the bones had evaporated from inside them, but I was home and alive.

For now.

Conrad and I were sitting at opposite ends of the sofa in my living room, both of us with cups of mint tea balanced in our laps. My mum was sitting in her chair, glaring at Conrad like she might take his cup from him and throw the contents in his face. Mom was pacing in front of the window, holding her own mug.

On the drive home, I'd messaged Freya and Ruby, telling them what had happened at Chalmers Hall, but they hadn't replied yet.

Then I'd confessed everything to my mothers: Ruby, Freya and me going back to Chalmers Hall on Freya's last night at home. Everything about the fake AltroWeb plan. All the way up to the moment Conrad O'Connell and I had dropped over the top of the wall and run towards their car, away from whoever was shooting at us.

My mothers hadn't spoken yet, stunned into silence by the appearance of a fugitive in their car. I'd fully expected them to drive us straight to the police station to hand Conrad in. But instead, we'd come home, my mom had locked the door and my mum made tea for everyone, including Conrad, without saying a single word.

"All right," my mum said at last. "Enough is enough."

My mom stopped pacing, and she, Conrad and I looked over at Mum.

"We need to call the police. We should have gone there straight away. We'll just have to hope they don't decide we're an accessory to harbouring a fugitive."

"Mum, you can't. We have a plan. I told you!" I said.

"To hell with your plan," my mum shouted. Her voice cracked as if she was close to tears. "Someone *shot* at you, Ivy. You could have been killed. Again."

Suddenly, she put her own mug down, rushed across the room and pulled me into her arms.

"Hold on," my mom said slowly.

Mum relaxed a bit, and I turned to my mom.

She was looking at Conrad with a frown on her face. "Last year, how did you and your aunt manage to get away from Chalmers Hall?" she asked him.

Conrad looked ashamed, staring at the cup in his hands.

"Dagmar was paying off the police. I don't know exactly who. If I did, I swear I'd tell you. All I know is she gave money to people pretty high up and regular officers too. They told her who was coming up for parole and who might be useful for her to recruit when they got out. They also looked away when Dagmar started bringing people in who were living on the streets." Conrad paused and swallowed loud enough that we could hear. "That's how we got away. Two separate police cars. She was put in one and me in another. I was let out near a private airfield a few towns away and told that Dagmar would meet me, but she never did. I lived on the streets until the heat died down, then I went back to Chalmers Hall."

"I knew it. Isn't that what Freya said too?" Mom asked me, but she didn't wait for an answer. "I knew someone in the police force had to be involved. If we call them, no doubt they'll take sonny boy here away, and he'll disappear. They won't find any evidence of bullets or anything at Chalmers Hall. The whole thing will be swept under the rug again."

"What are you saying?" my mum asked Mom, her face slack with shock.

Conrad and I looked at each other. I held my breath.

"I'm saying ..." Mom replied. "I can't believe I am saying it, but maybe, just maybe, their hare-brained scheme to catch *that woman* isn't the worst idea I've heard lately."

All of us – me, Mum and Conrad – gaped at my mom.

She was a *head teacher*. A public figure of authority. And here she was, practically agreeing with us.

But then again, Mom was the one who got really angry with politicians spinning their dead-cat stories to distract us from their lies. She was always furious when rich people weren't held to account for their crimes because they could buy their way out of trouble. All that stuff about fines only being a punishment if you were poor. My mom was an authority figure, but she was serious about that responsibility and hated when other people weren't.

"This isn't going to end until Dagmar Nilsson is locked up," my mom said. "And the only way that's going to happen is if she's caught in such a big way that no one can let her wriggle out of it. Not the police in her pockets, not even the politicians who pretend they're not making money from it. So we're going to throw a tech launch or whatever it is you were planning. If the police can't catch her, we'll simply have to do it ourselves."

"What?!" Mum, Conrad and I all shouted at the same time.

"That's amazing!" I added.

My mom turned to me, her eyes blazing. "Don't get excited just yet," she said fiercely. "First thing tomorrow, I'm going to call Ruby's mum and Freya's mum and stepdad and let them know what their daughters have been up to. You'd better hope I can get them on board with all this. And once the launch is over and Dagmar Nilsson is in prison, you're grounded until you're eighteen."

"Thirty," my mum corrected her.

"Thirty," Mom agreed. "Now get to bed. And I'll take your phone."

"What about Conrad?" I asked as I handed my phone to my mom.

"He can sleep on the sofa tonight. I'll stay down here with him," Mom said. "So don't get any ideas." She pointed at him.

Conrad flinched. "I won't, but you shouldn't let me stay," he said. "If the shooter comes here after me, you might be in danger too."

My mothers looked at each other.

"Do you think they'll come here?" Mum asked my mom.

"No," she said slowly. "Not tonight, at least. It's one thing to send an assassin to an abandoned house deep in the woods to kill a single fugitive boy. But it's another to order an assassin to a regular street in suburbia to kill a fugitive boy, a teenage girl, a therapist and a head teacher. *Especially* once it got out that Conrad and Ivy were two of the victims. It would shine a big spotlight straight back at Ms Nilsson, and I suspect that's the last thing she and her wealthy pals want. Even she would find it hard to hide from that level of attention. So for tonight, I think we're fine. We'll make a decision in the morning. Later in the morning," Mom amended, glancing at the clock.

"Ivy, you can sleep with me," my mum said. She was still holding me tightly.

"Mum, no."

"Mum, yes," she replied. "Be grateful I'm not handcuffing us together."

Conrad gave me a sympathetic glance as I left the living room, my mum's hand firm on my arm. But it was him I felt sorry for – Conrad was going to have to spend the night under the hawk eyes of my mom.

*

When I woke up the next morning, I was alone and confused about why I was in my parents' bed. Then everything from the night before came flooding back to me – trying to rescue Conrad, the person shooting at us, my mom embracing chaos. I flew out from under the covers, skidding onto the landing.

Down below, I could hear voices, lots of voices, all talking at once. Immediately, I was terrified my mothers had changed their minds and called the police. I raced down the stairs and threw the living-room door open.

Ruby and Mrs Brooks were sitting on the sofa. Freya's mum and stepdad were in each of the chairs my parents usually sat in. Conrad was on the floor by the radiator, my mum standing over him like a guard.

And in front of the television, looking ready for battle, was my mom.

Everyone stared at me. Ruby gave a small wave.

"Good. You're awake," my mom said. "As you can see, the cavalry is here. We've got a plan."

CHAPTER 11

A couple of weeks later, Ruby, Conrad, Freya and I were in Freya's living room, waiting for the doorbell to ring and for our special guests to arrive. From the kitchen, I could hear the chatter of our parents, plus Ella and Ella's Margot. They'd promised to stay out of the way while we met up with the most important part of our plan. But we all knew that as soon as the doorbell rang, they'd stop talking and start eavesdropping.

"I really didn't think I'd be back home so soon," Freya said.

She was standing by the window, half hiding behind the curtain. Conrad was on the floor, and Ruby and I were on the sofa.

"Sorry," I said.

"It's fine," Freya smiled. "I'd have hated it if you hadn't wanted me to come back and help. At least no one has shot at me. Yet," she added.

That part still didn't feel real. My mum had assigned me loads of therapy exercises so I could "process" it, but most of the time I felt fine. Honestly, I didn't think I could be seriously damaged any more, not after what happened at the Ash Tree Foundation.

However, on the drive over to Freya's, a car next to ours had backfired when the lights changed, and I'd lurched forward to hide in the footwell, thinking it was a gunshot. So maybe I did need a bit more processing.

"They're here," Freya said. "Oh god."

"Relax," Ruby said. She stood up and smoothed down her T-shirt. "It's going to be fine. They want to help, remember? They offered to come here and talk in person."

The doorbell rang, and Ruby headed for the front door.

"Deep breath. And … action …" I heard her mutter in the hall as she flung the door open. "Hi, it's so nice to meet you properly. I'm Ruby, obviously. Come in – the others are all waiting."

"It's so good to meet you too," a friendly voice replied to Ruby. "We're really glad to be able to help. Everything that woman has done is evil, so it's an honour to be part of this."

I looked at Freya. She'd turned the colour of bone. I patted the seat next to me, and she came over, allowing me to grab her hand and squeeze it.

A second later, Kim Hye-jin appeared in the doorway of Freya's living room.

She was followed by a tall Black boy, a few years older than me.

"Hi!" Hye-jin said, beaming at Conrad, who stood up to greet her.

The two of them hugged, and then Hye-jin turned to Freya.

"Hey, Freya," Hye-jin said. "Long time no see."

And then she opened her arms for a hug.

Freya stood and embraced her former best friend.

Last year, before everything went wrong at the Ash Tree Foundation, Conrad had told me that Hye-jin had almost been arrested because of Freya. Not that it was all Freya's fault. It was because of the AdelAIDE personal assistant, made by the Ash Tree Foundation. It had convinced

Freya to commit crimes for which Hye-jin had nearly got the blame. They hadn't spoken since, so Freya had been terrified when Conrad suggested that we contact Hye-jin for help, but it really was the only way to make our plan work.

We needed Kim Hye-jin on board because she was now dating Noah Watson. Noah was an eco-tech whizz-kid who'd just won an international award for developing a microchip. It was made using a sustainable and eco-friendly compound he'd invented *and* only cost a third of the standard market price to manufacture. He was the hottest thing in the technology world, and everyone wanted to work with him. Dagmar would know all of this, and of course she'd want him too.

Conrad said Noah was going to be a billionaire before he was twenty because of it.

My mom said we'd better work with Noah before that happened and he turned evil.

"Noah, it's so good to meet you in person," Ruby said. "Come in – sit down. Let's get *Operation Takedown*'s first meeting under way."

Conrad and I exchanged a quick smile at Ruby's codename.

Hye-jin released Freya and moved to Noah's side. The two of them lowered themselves to the floor, sitting cross-legged. Conrad, Freya and Ruby did the same, so I scooted down from the sofa, completing the circle.

"All right," Noah began. "Here's where we're at. Hye-jin and I shot the video this morning. In it, I said I was excited to announce my partnership with AltroWeb and would be at the launch tomorrow and after that I'd explain more. The video is scheduled to drop in an hour, which means Dagmar will have loads of time to see it and convince one of her rich friends to lend her a private jet to get here."

We all looked at the clock over the fireplace, then turned back to Noah.

He continued, "My buddies are happy to lend us their offices in Silicon Fen – that's the part of Cambridge where a lot of the tech companies are – for the launch. They're going to swap out their logos for the AltroWeb ones and make it look legit. They've been sending me photos all morning."

Noah paused and opened the chat on his phone, scrolling slowly so we could see the work his friends were doing.

"It looks amazing," Conrad said. "Completely real."

We all murmured our agreement.

"I'll tell them you like it," Noah said, tapping out a message, then putting his phone away.

"They're also going to stick around and pretend to be part of the company," Noah said. "They don't know it's a sting operation – they think it's a prank I'm playing on someone."

"Won't they be annoyed when they find out you lied to them?" I asked.

"Maybe for a minute, but then I'll offer to partner with them on some solar-panel tech they're developing and hopefully they'll forgive me." Noah grinned. Then he added, "For the record, I was planning to work with them anyway. That's why they're so keen to help me out. Plus, it'll be great publicity for them and a hell of a story to tell at parties. It'll be cool – don't worry."

"Good," Ruby said. "Some of my friends from my performing arts group will be there, working as catering staff. My mum is actually going to cater it, so it'll be good food."

"My stepdad has asked a bunch of his friends from work to come along and mill about in suits, pretending to be investors," Freya said quietly. "He had to tell them the plan, but all of them were given AdelAIDE units to test too, and they all had problems with them. Their ones weren't as unhinged as mine, but they were still furious the company got away with it."

"And I'll be there as bait," I said.

It was the part of the plan my mothers hated most, but we'd already convinced Dagmar that Conrad had recruited me. He couldn't be there because he was wanted by the police too, but I could be, and it would make it all seem real.

"Anything else?" Ruby asked.

"Actually, yes," Conrad said.

I stared at him, but he wouldn't look back at me.

Conrad took a deep breath. "I'm going to be there as bait too."

"You can't," I reminded him. "You'll get arrested when the police come."

Conrad turned to me. "I know. But I need to pay for what I've done, Ivy. If I don't, what kind of life can I have? I can't stay on the run for ever, with you bringing me pasta salad and socks."

Opposite us, I saw Hye-jin and Noah exchange a glance. I ignored them, focusing on Conrad.

"Besides," he went on, "I want to be there when this ends, not sitting in a room far away, watching it."

"Like us chumps," Ruby muttered.

"I've made up my mind," Conrad said.

I knew he was right.

And I had to admit, Conrad being there would definitely draw Dagmar out.

"All right. If you're sure," I said.

Conrad nodded.

"Then I guess we're all sorted," I said, smiling at him.

"You can come in now!" Ruby bellowed in the direction of the kitchen. Suddenly, the room filled with adults, all of them making a beeline for Hye-jin and Noah to say hello.

Ruby, Freya, Conrad and I stepped back, heading out to the kitchen.

"So this is really happening," Freya said.

"It's really happening," Ruby confirmed. "This time tomorrow, it might all be over."

I looked at Conrad.

He nodded at me. "Let's hope so," he said.

*

The following afternoon, Conrad and I stood in the AltroWeb offices in Silicon Fen.

The logo Freya had designed had been stencilled onto the longest wall, right in the middle: a gigantic spiderweb like a target with an eye in the centre of it. On the far wall there was a rotating projection of the logo, just like on the website, beaming onto the plain white surface. Laptops had been left open on desks, all of them displaying the logo too. As if that wasn't enough, Ruby's drama-group friends were milling about holding trays of food and drinks, wandering between Noah's tech pals and Freya's dad's colleagues. At the heart of the room stood Noah and Hye-jin, with everyone trying to get near them and talk to them.

There was a real sense of excitement in the air. I'd never been to the launch of anything before, but what Noah's friend's had done – what we'd all done here – felt really special. It felt real.

"You OK?" Conrad asked.

"Are you?" I asked. "You're the one who's going to spend tonight in jail if this goes well."

Conrad grinned, surprisingly chipper. "But I won't be the *only* one in jail if this goes well. And I suppose I'd better make the most of my freedom while I can."

He snagged a canapé and a glass of champagne from a passing actor/waiter.

"I'm eighteen, so it's legal," Conrad said, and then took a large swig.

"Conrad, over here!" Noah called, waving him over.

Conrad looked at me. "Go," I said. "I'm going to mingle."

I watched Conrad walk over to where Noah was standing with some of his friends. They were laughing and looking like they really were having a great party.

I moved back into the shadows, watching the spinning logo on the wall at the far end of the room. The room was starting to fill up, and music was on – something I didn't recognise. Noah had said it would probably get busy like this as the companies and offices nearby heard there was a party and came to see what the fuss was about. Not to mention all the people who wanted to befriend him and get access to Noah's miracle chip. He'd told Ruby's mum to cater for double the amount of people we'd told her would be there, and he'd cover the costs, no worries.

My mothers had wanted Noah to hire private security to make sure no one could bring a weapon in. But I'd pointed out to them that any visible security might put off Dagmar from trying to get in, and we wanted her trapped in *our* web before she realised what was really going on. They'd backed down, and I hoped they were OK about it. Noah had sweet-talked a company in the building across the road to let all the parents wait there while the sting operation happened. Ruby's mum was with us, as the catering boss, but she was trying to keep a low profile in the back, just in case someone recognised her.

I watched people milling about, and then I noticed a man standing by the big windows on the opposite side of the room from me. He was talking hurriedly on his phone.

Something about him caught my attention. I knew him from somewhere.

Another man walked over to him, and the two of them began peering around the room.

Their eyes locked on me.

At that exact moment, it hit me.

They were from the Ash Tree Foundation.

The first man, the one on his phone, had been guarding the attic the first night I stayed at Chalmers Hall. He was the person who'd sent me down to Dagmar's office.

The second man was the one who came to fetch Conrad while we were having dinner the night I sneaked out of the Foundation and found the folly.

They were here.

Which meant Dagmar—

Something hard pressed into the base of my spine.

"Don't scream," Dagmar Nilsson said into my ear. "Don't make any kind of fuss. Just walk. Or my man on the roof above shoots your mothers. That is them in the building opposite, isn't it?"

CHAPTER 12

As soon as Dagmar had got me out of the room, she went into my pocket and took out my phone. She threw it to the ground and stamped on it.

"Walk," Dagmar said again, and I did, until we reached a door.

Dagmar opened it and shoved me inside, following me in and closing the door after us.

I turned to face her.

Her white-blonde hair was gone, dyed a plain brown now. She wasn't wearing white either – instead, she was dressed in a black skirt and waistcoat over a white shirt. She'd dressed up like one of the catering staff.

"Now, tell me the truth," Dagmar said. "This chip that Noah boy has been working on with AltroWeb – what does it do?"

In her hand, the gun shook slightly.

Dagmar was scared, I realised. And somehow that made me feel braver.

"It's like Novo Reality, but you wear it inside you. In your head," I said.

My voice was steady, and I started improvising. It wouldn't be long before someone would realise I wasn't there – Noah, or Hye-jin, or Conrad, or Ruby's mum. They'd raise the alarm and come looking. I just had to stay cool until then. Back when I played my games, I was always good at holding my nerve until the battle with the main boss was over. It was just a matter of staying focused. Keeping your eyes on the prize.

I looked at Dagmar and kept talking.

"It's organic. Noah invented something that means it's really eco-friendly. It—"

"I don't care about that!" Dagmar hissed. "Tell me what it does. Have you used it?"

"Not yet," I said. "But there's going to be a full demo later, using a skin patch with the chip inside, and I've offered to do it because I was so good at Novo Reality."

"Shut up," Dagmar commanded. "Where is the patch? The one they're using for the demo. Does that Noah boy have it on him?"

"No," I scoffed. "It's way too valuable. It's in the safe."

A glint entered Dagmar's eye. "Where's the safe?" she asked.

"In the office. Down the hall," I added when she jerked the gun at me. "But there's a security guard in there."

"Just one?"

I nodded. "Noah didn't want them at the party because he said they'd ruin the vibe," I lied. "But the AltroWeb people insisted the chip had security, so Noah said fine, but then the chip had to stay in the office until the big moment."

Ruby would be very proud of me, a little voice in my head said. I was acting my heart out here.

Dagmar gave me an appraising look. "You know, I was convinced this was all part of some juvenile plan when Conrad first posted his video. I honestly didn't think you had it in you. Either of you." She paused and then narrowed her eyes wickedly. "Well, maybe I thought you did. It was

Conrad saying you were involved that made me pay attention. I know just how much you loved Novo Reality. How long did it take you to stop dreaming about it? Or do you still dream you're in there, back in the folly, plugged in, making a world all of your own?"

Fear began to creep into my mind.

"I don't think about it at all," I said, but now there was a shake to my voice. A cold sweat had broken out over my chest.

"Liar," Dagmar whispered. "I know you, Ivy Finch. You're exactly who I'm building the new world for."

She poked the gun into my belly.

"Let's go and get our future, shall we?" she said. "Turn around."

I did as she asked. Dagmar jammed the gun into my back, leaning against me as she opened the door a crack.

"Walk," she said.

I'd taken two steps when I heard someone call out "Ivy?" behind me.

Before I could say anything, the pressure against my spine was gone and a loud bang had split the corridor in two.

My ears were ringing so hard I lost my balance. I fell to the floor as two large shapes shot past me.

On my hands and knees, I turned round and saw Dagmar's face. It was red and furious, pressed into the carpet, distorted by a scream the ringing drowned out. She locked eyes with me and said something I was grateful I couldn't hear.

Two men were holding Dagmar down, one pulling her arms behind her back and putting her wrists into metal handcuffs. She was being arrested. She was really being arrested.

We'd done it.

And then I saw beyond her.

Conrad O'Connell was lying on the carpet in a pool of blood.

Suddenly, my mothers were there, and the corridor was full of people, and I couldn't see Conrad any more.

I tried to ask my mom if Conrad was OK, but my mouth wouldn't work, and my legs wouldn't work. It was like just after I'd been rescued from the folly, when my body wouldn't obey me any more.

Then I was in an ambulance, then at hospital, and none of the doctors or nurses would tell me what had happened. My hearing slowly came back, and my legs and arms started to work again.

"You were in shock, that's all," a nurse said to me. "Aural shock from the gunshot and physical shock from the ordeal. You've been so brave."

"But what about Conrad?" I asked. "Is he all right?"

"Your mothers want to see you," the nurse replied. "I'll send them in."

A few seconds later, my mom and mum were rushing towards me.

"Is Conrad alive?" I begged them.

EPILOGUE

Conrad is fine. Dagmar's shot clipped him in the arm, causing a lot of bleeding but not enough to kill him. Just enough to make Conrad faint, which is why I'd seen him collapsed on the ground.

Apparently, lots of people had told me this, repeatedly, but I didn't really understand it. The thankfully temporary damage to my ears from the gunshot and my general shock stopped me from absorbing it. It only sank in when my mothers wheeled me into the room where Conrad was being bandaged up under the careful watch of two police officers.

Dagmar is in a high-security prison awaiting trial. Not because she is considered dangerous but because she ratted out every single politician and police commissioner and millionaire who'd helped her cover up what she'd done, and who'd opened doors for her in return for a share of the profits. She did it to save herself, but in trying to weasel her way *out* of trouble, she landed herself in the biggest trouble of her life. There is nowhere in the world Dagmar can hide now, nowhere she'll be safe.

My mom smiled about it so much that her face started to hurt, and my mum told her to pull herself together.

Conrad was arrested and charged, but he was given a suspended sentence – because he'd been a minor when Dagmar got him involved in all the Ash Tree Enterprises stuff, and because he'd worked so hard to try to catch her, even risking his life to save mine.

He's living back with his mum now and thinking about applying to university. We still speak every day. I think Conrad would like to be more than friends with me, but to be honest, I really want a quiet life for a bit. No drama of any kind, unless Ruby is doing it.

Freya is really happy at university. She changed her course at the last minute to robotics, of all things, plus something I don't really understand called mechatronics engineering. Once she's finished, there's a job waiting for her at Noah Watson's brand-new company, BeneVista.

Noah sold the patent to his miracle chip for one pound so no one could ever become a billionaire from it. He's also made all the resources that helped him develop it open source so anyone can use them too.

"If this big tech wave is coming, then I want to understand it," Freya told me and Ruby on a video call the night before her course started. "Understand it and be able to direct it. Look at Noah. He's proof there are good people in the tech world – people who are in it for more than the money and power. I want to be like him. Saving the world with eco-tech."

As for Ruby, she'd been hoping someone would want to buy the rights to our lives to make a film about what had happened to us, and play herself in the movie. She was very disappointed when no one did. But like I said to her, it's probably for the best – what actor wants to be typecast as themselves?

I think Ruby will get over it eventually. Or she'll use it as motivation.

Either way, I think we're all going to be OK now.

Our books are tested
for children and young people by
children and young people.

Thanks to everyone who consulted on
a manuscript for their time and effort in
helping us to make our books better
for our readers.